This book belongs to

~~Ryley~~ Rochelle

Published in 2007 by Igloo Books Ltd
Cottage Farm, Sywell, NN6 0BJ
www.igloo-books.com

10 9 8 7 6 5

ISBN: 978 1 84561 0876

Printed in China

The Tooth Fairy

igloo

One starry, moonlit night Fairyland Forest was alive with the tinkle of tiny voices and the whisper of fluttering wings. It was the night of the fairy gathering, when fairies from all over the kingdom came before Queen Isabella to voice their troubles and woes. It was a very important occasion and everyone was there. Everyone, that is, except for Sparkle, the tooth fairy. Sparkle was still on her rounds, gathering the baby teeth that had fallen out of the mouths of little girls and boys that day. Sparkle loved little children and adored her job, but it did mean she was always late!

A sudden hush fell over the forest, as in a glittering flash of fairy dust Queen Isabella appeared before the waiting fairies. "Are we all here?" she asked in a voice as sweet as honey and as light as a fairy's wing.

"Not quite," said one little fairy, stepping into the fairy ring. It was Trixie, the problem-solving fairy. "My best friend, Sparkle, is still hard at work. She is the tooth fairy. She collects all the baby teeth children lose just before they get their grown-up teeth. She never knows where she's going to find one, so she has to search every nook and cranny. It takes a very long time."

When Trixie had finished, a very important looking fairy with a big stick stood before the Queen and banged the ground three times. "Let the meeting begin," she announced.

The first fairy to come before the Queen was Zoe, the sewing fairy. She told everyone how she had made too many fairy bags and didn't know what to do with them.

Then, while everyone puzzled over that problem, Ursula, the potion fairy, stood up.

"I've run out of sparkles," she explained. "Without sparkles, I can't make fairy dust, and without fairy dust there is no magic. We've just got to find something sparkly, pure and good to make more sparkles!"

Ursula had barely finished speaking, when a wretched looking creature flopped down in the centre of the fairy ring. It was a very tired and dirty-looking Sparkle. She'd had a hard night searching for baby teeth beneath dusty beds and grimy floorboards.

"I heard that," she panted. "And I've got just the thing." Sparkle reached into the bulging sack she was carrying and pulled out something that sparkled in the moonlight. "Baby teeth," she explained. "What could be more pure and good? And just look at that sparkle!"

Everyone, including Queen Isabella, agreed that
it was a perfect solution.

"And I've had an idea for Zoe's fairy bags,"
announced Trixie. "We can give them to all the little
children to put their fallen baby teeth in. Then they
can put the bag under their pillow. That way,
Sparkle won't have to spend so much time searching
for lost teeth."

Sparkle nodded her head enthusiastically. "I think it would be nice if we left the children a reward for their teeth, too," she added. "After all, without them we wouldn't have any fairy dust."

"Hear, hear!" cried Queen Isabella enthusiastically. And so it was agreed.

The following day, before Sparkle flew off into the night, the fairies gathered together to write letters to all the little children in the world. As all the other fairies scribbled away, Sparkle told them what to write.

Dear . . . .
(write your own name here)

Don't worry if a baby tooth begins to wobble, then falls out. Put it in this little pouch and pop it under your pillow when you go to bed. While you are sleeping, I will take it away and leave you a coin in its place. Don't worry about the gap your missing baby tooth leaves, a brand new tooth will soon grow to fill it.

Lots of love,

Sparkle
The Tooth Fairy

When the letters were written, all the fairies helped
Sparkle deliver them, along with the fairy bags.

And from that day forth, Sparkle was never late for anything again because her job was much, much easier. All the little children put their baby teeth in their pouches and placed them under their pillows where Sparkle could find them. Never again did she have to scramble under beds or between floorboards. Sparkle was a very happy fairy.

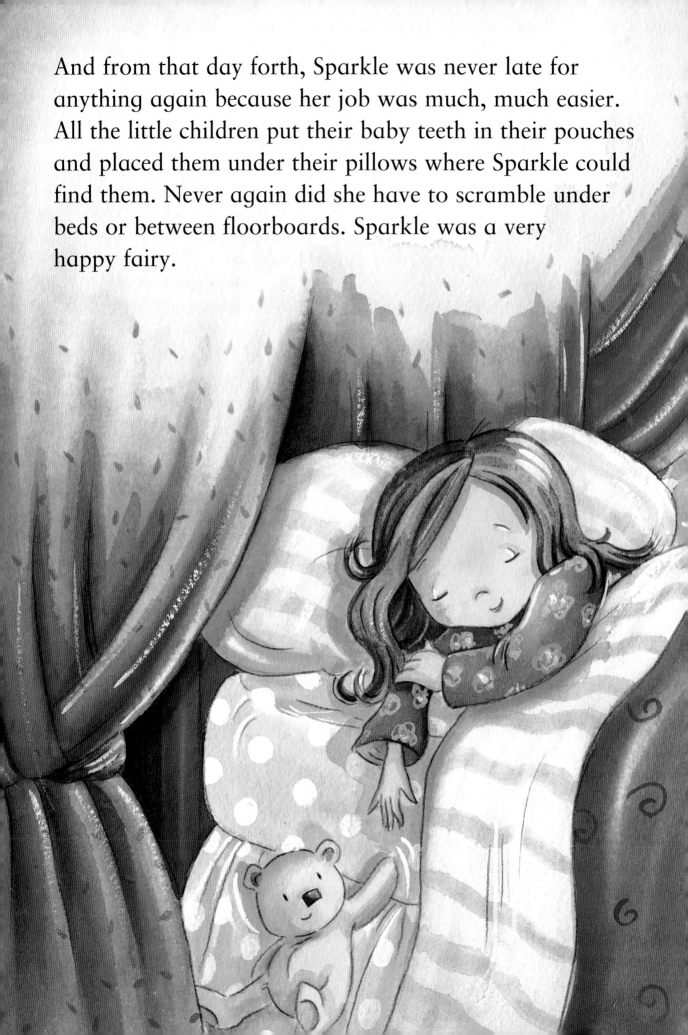

And Sparkle wasn't the only one who was happy. Zoe was happy because all her lovely bags were being used. Ursula was happy because she had lots and lots of gorgeous sparkles for her fairy dust. Queen Isabella and the rest of the fairies were happy because they had lots of lovely fairy dust to do magical things with.

But, best of all, the little children were happy because
they knew that if they looked after their baby teeth, and
cleaned them regularly, they would get a reward whenever
one fell out!

All About My Teeth

The chart below shows the position of all the baby teeth in
your mouth. You can keep a record of your teeth, by colouring
in each baby tooth when it falls out, and writing down
the date on the opposite page.

My Tooth Chart